For Isabella, past and present —TSS

For Mom and Dad —MG

ABOUT THIS BOOK

The illustrations for this book were done in watercolor and mixed media. This book was edited by Susan Rich and designed by Saho Fujii. The production was supervised by Virginia Lawther, and the production editor was Marisa Finkelstein. The text was set in Carre Noir Light, and the display type is Bach Black.

Text copyright © 2021 by Tasha Spillett-Sumner ★ Illustrations copyright © 2021 by Michaela Goade ★ Cover illustration © 2021 by Michaela Goade. Cover design by Neil Swaab and Saho Fujii ★ Cover copyright © 2021 by Hachette Book Group, Inc. ★ Hachette Book Group supports the right to free expression and the value of copyright. The purpose of copyright is to encourage writers and artists to produce the creative works that enrich our culture. ★ The scanning, uploading, and distribution of this book without permission is a theft of the author's intellectual property. If you would like permission to use material from the book (other than for review purposes), please contact permissions@hbgusa.com. Thank you for your support of the author's rights. ★ Little, Brown and Company ★ Hachette Book Group ★ 1290 Avenue of the Americas, New York, NY 10104 ★ Visit us at LBYR.com ★ First Edition: April 2021 ★ Little, Brown and Company is a division of Hachette Book Group, Inc. ★ The Little, Brown name and logo are trademarks of Hachette Book Group, Inc. ★ The publisher is not responsible for websites (or their content) that are not owned by the publisher. ★ Library of Congress Cataloging-in-Publication Data ★ Names: Spillett-Sumner, Tasha, 1988– author. | Goade, Michaela, illustrator. ★ Title: I sang you down from the stars / by Tasha Spillett-Sumner ; art by Michaela Goade. ★ Description: First edition. | New York : Little, Brown and Company, 2021. | Audience: Ages 4–8. | Summary: A Native American woman describes how she loved her child before it was born and, throughout her pregnancy, gathered a bundle of gifts to welcome the newborn. Identifiers: LCCN 2020005062 | ISBN 9780316493161 (hardcover) ★ Subjects: CYAC: Babies— Fiction. | Mother and child—Fiction. | Native Americans—Fiction. ★ Classification: LCC PZ7.1.S7147 Iah 2021 | DDC [E]—dc23 LC record available at https://lccn.loc.gov/2020005062 ★ ISBN 978-0-316-49316-1 ★ PRINTED IN CHINA ★ APS ★ 10 9 8 7 6 5 4 3 2

I Sang You Down from the Stars

from the

Written by
Tasha Spillett-Sumner

Illustrated by
Michaela Goade

L B

Little, Brown and Company
New York Boston

I loved you before I met you.
Before I held you in my arms,
I sang you down from the stars.

As I searched for your eyes in the sky,
I saw a shooting star.
I followed it to a fluffy white eagle plume.
I held on to it. The first gift in a bundle
that will be yours.

Summer was fading into fall on the day I found out that you had chosen to make my body your first home.

Together we went to gather cedar and sage, medicines that will keep our spirits strong through the winter.
When you are old enough, I will teach you how to use them.

Into your bundle they go.

As the Northwind blew,
you grew bigger and stronger.

Waiting for you taught me
about patience and love.

With care in my hands, I sewed your first star blanket. With each stitch, I whispered a prayer for you and thought about wrapping you up warm and safe, just like you are now in my belly.

Into your bundle it goes.

As the ice began to melt, we visited the river.
When our people travel the waterways, the song
of the rushing rapids calls us home.
I picked up a small stone for you, so that you always
remember you belong to this place.

Into your bundle it goes.

You arrived in the spring, with the waters that come
when the ice breaks and the rivers flow again.
For the first time, after our long wait, I looked down
at you and found stars in your eyes.
Our hearts danced together.

I honored your journey from the Sky by passing on
the gifts I had gathered for you. This, my baby, is your
sacred medicine bundle.

First, I wrapped you in your star blanket
and held you close to me.

The fluffy plume I found when I followed the shooting star is a reminder that there is beauty all around us; we just have to look and see.

Medicines of cedar and sage are for you to keep your spirit strong.

When you hold this stone from the river, remember that
the Land carries stories, and so do you.

Family and friends came from near
and far to welcome you.

One by one,
they held you and greeted you.

You brought them so much love and joy.
I saw that you, my baby, are also a
sacred bundle.

You are my baby bundle.

As I held you close, I whispered in your ear,
"I loved you before I met you.
Before I held you in my arms,
I sang you down from the stars."

A NOTE FROM THE AUTHOR

This story lived in my head long before it found a home on the page, much like the prayer for my daughter lived in my heart long before she found a home in my womb.

I Sang You Down from the Stars shines a light on the traditional understanding of my Nation, the Inniniwak, and many other Indigenous peoples globally: that babies choose their parents. It also shows the mindful preparation that is involved in getting ready to welcome a baby into a family and a community.

As the child and the mother grow with each other, sacred items are collected on the child's behalf. These sacred items will make up the child's medicine bundle. Within a traditional medicine bundle, each item collected is intended to help keep the child's connection to their identity strong. The items are bundled together to create something that the child can carry and lean on through their life journey.

The baby arrives with their own gifts to bestow, among them love and understanding, and the promise of carrying on the traditions of family and community imbued with a sense of belonging to their traditional territory. In this way, a baby is also a sacred bundle.

My hope is that this book will find its way into homes where babies are being welcomed with similar gifts of love, strength, and belonging.

A NOTE FROM THE ARTIST

There is so much magic in life, so much spirit in everything around us. You can find it in the waters that flow around and within us; in the stars that wink above; in trees, rocks, and animals; and in the dreams we send out to the world. Everything has spirit. For this book, I wanted to visualize this, to create a flow of energy that connects all living things on a metaphorical level and connects from one page to the next on a literal level. My editor, Susan Rich, and I affectionately named this visual element "the swoosh."

I found inspiration in the gathering and gifting themes of this story. When each gift is bestowed on the baby, the corresponding gathering spread from earlier in the book is referenced through imagery, colors, message, and often through the swoosh itself. In this way, the teachings and hopes for the child come full circle. The swoosh helps us visualize the connections to land, culture, family, and identity.